Negation

BAPTISM
OF FIRE

Publisher's Cataloging-in-Publication Data
(Prepared by The Donohue Group, Inc.)

  Negation. Volume two : baptism of fire / Writer: Tony Bedard ; Penciler: Paul Pelletier ; Inker: David
Meikis ; Colorist: James Rochelle.

   p. : ill. ; cm.

   Spine title: Negation. 2 : baptism of fire

   ISBN: 1-931484-59-7

1. Science fiction. 2. Adventure fiction. 3. Graphic novels. 4. Kaine (Fictitious character)--Fiction.
5. Evinlea (Fictitious character)--Fiction. 6. Matua (Fictitious character)--Fiction. 7. Zaida (Fictitious
character)--Fiction. I. Bedard, Tony. II. Pelletier, Paul. III. Meikis, David. IV. Rochelle, James. V.
Title: Baptism of fire VI. Title: Negation. 4 : baptism of fire.

PN6728 .N44 2002
813.54 [Fic]

NEGATION®

BAPTISM OF FIRE

Tony **BEDARD**
W R I T E R

Paul **PELLETIER**
P E N C I L E R

David **MEIKIS**
I N K E R

James **ROCHELLE**
C O L O R I S T

CHAPTER II
Yanick **PAQUETTE** · PENCILER
Drew **GERACI** · INKER
Justin **THYME** · COLORIST

Troy **PETERI** · LETTERER

CrossGeneration Comics   Oldsmar, Florida

BAPTISM OF FIRE

features Chapters 7-12
of the ongoing series
NEGATION

The God-Emperor **Charon** conquered His chaotic universe and forged an intergalactic empire known as:

THE
NEGATION

But omnipotence is not enough. Charon now covets the bright and thriving worlds in our cosmos.

On His orders, one hundred strangers were abducted from our universe and brought to His dark realm to be tortured and tested… to struggle and die. Some, like the healer **Javi** and the constable **Shassa**, bear a mysterious mark of power known as the **Sigil**, which gives them superhuman abilities. Others hail from inherently powerful races, such as **Evinlea** of the godlike First, the tattooed **Matua**, who comes from a world of magicians, and the reptilian warrior known simply as the **Lizard Lady.** Most of Charon's captives, however, are simple, ordinary humans.

One such human named **Obregon Kaine** led an uprising against the Negation prison warden, **Komptin**. Two separate groups of prisoners escaped — some with Kaine, others with the space-pirate, **Mercer Drake**. Both groups wandered the hostile stars, seeking a way home.

Kaine and his companions encountered **Captain Fluxor**, a local explorer also on the run from the Empire who now serves as their guide to Negation Space. Meanwhile, Komptin pursued Kaine with such single-minded hatred that he risked petitioning the help of **Lawbringer Qztr** — Charon's most dreaded enforcer.

After several harrowing weeks, Kaine and company ended up on the same planet as Drake's team. Now, Kaine's comrades, who blame the other escapees for leaving them to die back on the prison world, finally have their chance to give Drake a little payback…

"...FOR I KNOW WELL THAT IT IS A PLACE OF *SORROW* AND *STRIFE*."

EVINLEA... *WAIT*...

NO, DRAKE. NO *EXCUSES*, NO *APPEALS*.

YOU *SEALED* YOUR FATE WHEN YOU LEFT ME TO *DIE* IN THAT PRISON.

Y'KNOW... ⇒*UNH*⇐ ...I COULD PROBABLY...*TALK* SOME SENSE INTO YOU...

...BUT IT WON'T *FEEL* AS GOOD...

TOO BAD. WE *COUNTED* ON YOU TO SECURE THAT PRISON TRANSPORT FOR *ALL* OF US.

DO YOU HAVE ANY IDEA WHAT IT *FELT* LIKE, WATCHING YOU FLY AWAY WHILE THE WHOLE PLANET WENT UP IN *FLAMES* AROUND US?!

MONCHITO, MONCHI*TO!*

WHAT THE HELL IS *GOING ON* HERE? WE THOUGHT WE HEARD *EXPLOSIONS...*

SHASSA! WHAT...WHAT ARE *THEY* DOING HERE?

IT'S *EASY* TO KICK A MAN WHEN HE'S DOWN. HOW ABOUT A *REAL* CHALLENGE?

DON'T BE RIDICULOUS. EVEN HOBBLED BY THIS CURSED COSMOS, I AM STILL A HUNDRED TIMES *STRONGER* THAN YOU.

I'LL TELL YOU WHAT THEY'RE *NOT* DOING: *LISTENING...*

...BUT *I* KNOW HOW TO GET SOMEONE'S *ATTENTION...*

YOU! GET BACK HERE, OR I'LL *SHOOT!*

YOU DON'T KNOW A *THING* ABOUT ME.

I TAKE IT SHE'S BEEN *PRACTICING*...?

WE *ALL* HAVE. WE'VE FOUND THE MORE WE USE OUR *SIGILS* IN NEGATION SPACE, THE BETTER THEY WORK.

YOU JUST CAN'T BITE OFF TOO MUCH AT FIRST.

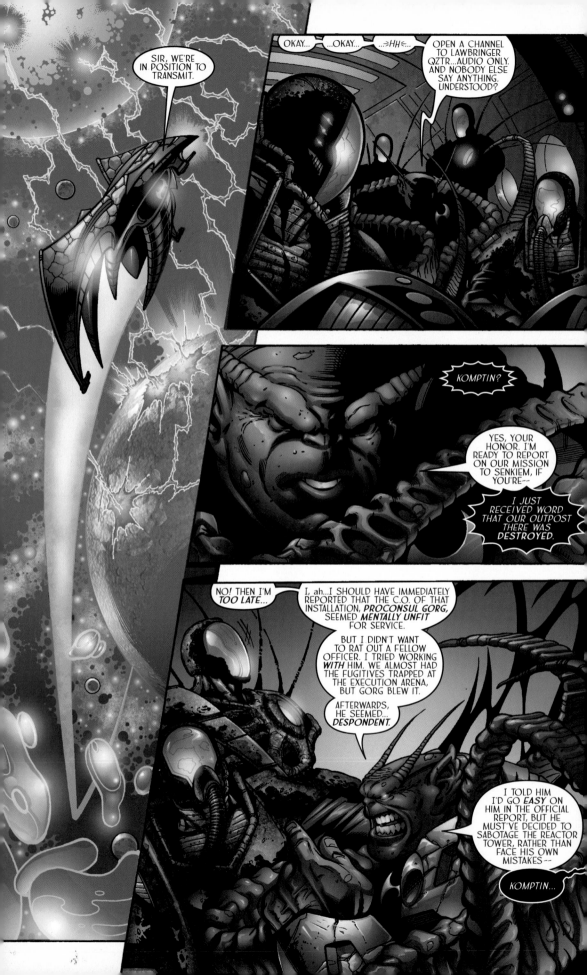

DO YOU...DO YOU KNOW *WHERE* THE ESCAPEES TELEPORTED TO?

YES, BUT THAT IS NO LONGER YOUR CONCERN. I SHALL ATTEND TO THEM *MYSELF.*

ASSUME A STANDARD PATROL OF THIS SECTOR AND AWAIT FURTHER

I DON'T *BELIEVE* IT!

WE'RE *ALIVE!*

THAT WAS *BRAVE,* TAKING THE BLAME LIKE YOU DID.

YOU MUST BE THE *LUCKIEST--*

YOU IDIOTS!

DON'T YOU *SEE?!* I *CAN'T* LET HIM GO KILL *KAINE* AND THE OTHERS...

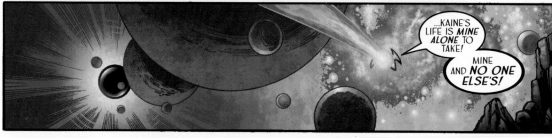

...KAINE'S LIFE IS *MINE ALONE* TO TAKE!

MINE AND *NO ONE ELSE'S!*

...ALL I WAS TRYING TO DO WAS START THE ENGINES! I DIDN'T MEAN TO *LEAVE* YOU GUYS, BUT THE WHOLE LAUNCH SEQUENCE WAS *AUTOMATED!*

YEAH, WE HAD OUR *OWN* AUTO-LAUNCH DISASTER ON THE LAST PLANET WE-- oh, NO...

EVINLEA! STOP IT BEFORE YOU GET *HURT!*

YOU, um, LOOK *DIFFERENT,* DON'T YOU..?

?

KROM

ALL RIGHT, I THINK OUR SHIP CAN STILL ACCOMMODATE EVERY ONE OF US.

EVINLEA, I--

SHUT UP.

IN SPITE OF WHAT JUST HAPPENED, I CAN'T SAY HOW *GLAD* I AM THAT THERE WERE *MORE* SURVIVORS FROM OUR JAILBREAK.

I'M NOT SURE WHO KNEW WHOM BACK IN THE PRISON, SO IF EVERYBODY WOULDN'T MIND *INTRODUCING* THEMSELVES...?

MERCER DRAKE.

IRESS, OF HOUSE DEXTER.

AGLAREB OF GRINBOR.

I'M *CALYX* OF TORBEL. AND THIS IS *FOONIE.*

MONCHITO.

QUOLZAG.

WU PING LAM.

'ERE, WOT'S *THIS* BLEEDIN' BILGE...?

THUSTRA.

BLIMEY!

SKLUTCH!

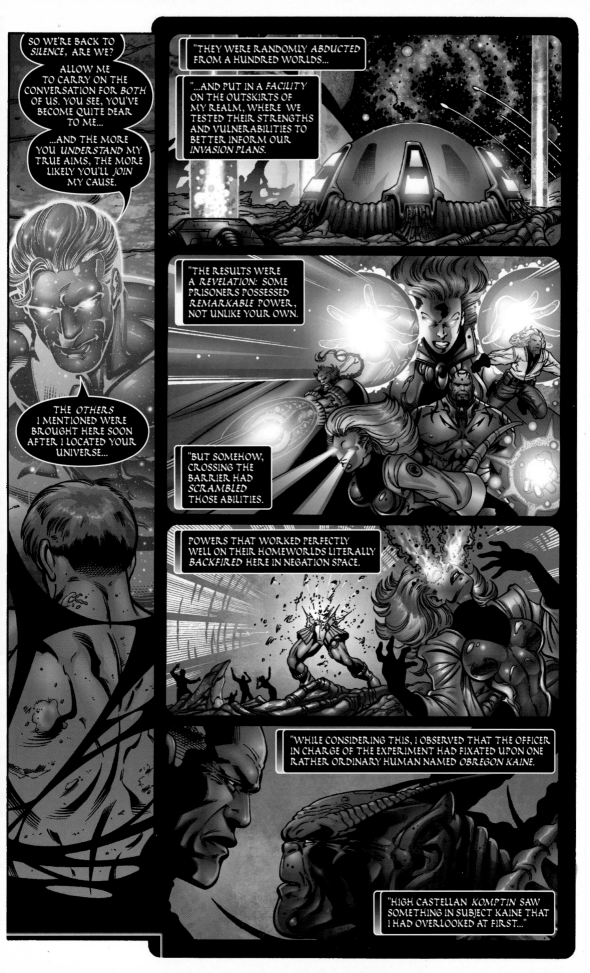

SO WE'RE BACK TO *SILENCE*, ARE WE?

ALLOW ME TO CARRY ON THE CONVERSATION FOR *BOTH* OF US. YOU SEE, YOU'VE BECOME QUITE DEAR TO ME...

...AND THE MORE YOU *UNDERSTAND MY TRUE AIMS*, THE MORE LIKELY YOU'LL *JOIN MY CAUSE*.

THE *OTHERS* I MENTIONED WERE BROUGHT HERE SOON AFTER I LOCATED YOUR UNIVERSE...

"THEY WERE RANDOMLY *ABDUCTED* FROM A HUNDRED WORLDS...

"...AND PUT IN A *FACILITY* ON THE OUTSKIRTS OF MY REALM, WHERE WE TESTED THEIR STRENGTHS AND VULNERABILITIES TO BETTER INFORM OUR *INVASION PLANS*.

"THE RESULTS WERE A *REVELATION*: SOME PRISONERS POSSESSED *REMARKABLE* POWER, NOT UNLIKE YOUR OWN.

"BUT SOMEHOW, CROSSING THE BARRIER HAD *SCRAMBLED* THOSE ABILITIES.

POWERS THAT WORKED PERFECTLY WELL ON THEIR HOMEWORLDS LITERALLY *BACKFIRED* HERE IN NEGATION SPACE.

"WHILE CONSIDERING THIS, I OBSERVED THAT THE OFFICER IN CHARGE OF THE EXPERIMENT HAD FIXATED UPON ONE RATHER ORDINARY HUMAN NAMED *OBREGON KAINE*.

"HIGH CASTELLAN *KOMPTIN* SAW SOMETHING IN SUBJECT KAINE THAT I HAD OVERLOOKED AT FIRST..."

THE ONE NAMED *EVINLEA* WILL STEP FORWARD AND DEPART WITH ME.

THE REST OF YOU WILL *REMAIN* HERE AND...

...AND...

WHAT?

WHAT *IS* IT?

Oh.

BUT *WHAT?*

WELL, SIR, WE'RE ALL WONDERING WHY WE'RE *HERE.* LAWBRINGER QZTR ORDERED US TO MAINTAIN A PATROL TWO SECTORS AWAY.

SIR, WE'VE ESTABLISHED CONTACT WITH THE CIVIL COMM-SYSTEM ON KALIMA, BUT...

AS SOON AS QZTR GETS TIRED OF PLAYING WITH THE FUGITIVES, HE'LL CALL US IN TO COLLECT WHOEVER'S LEFT ALIVE. WHEN HE DOES, IF PRISONER KAINE IS STILL BREATHING...WELL...

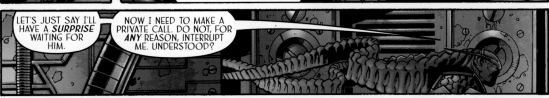

LET'S JUST SAY I'LL HAVE A *SURPRISE* WAITING FOR HIM.

NOW I NEED TO MAKE A PRIVATE CALL. DO NOT, FOR *ANY* REASON, INTERRUPT ME. UNDERSTOOD?

⇒HH⇐

OH, FOR CHARON'S SAKE...

PEEP PEEP PEEP

CALL BACK -- I'M *BUSY!*

THAT'S A HELL OF A WAY TO ANSWER THE PHONE, *KAMFIR.*

PUT *MOTHER* ON.

KOMPTIN? IS THAT YOU?! WHAT ARE **YOU** CALLING FOR?

I **TOLD** YOU I WANT TO SPEAK WITH MOTHER.

FORGET IT. I AM **THIS** CLOSE TO BEATING MY TOP SCORE. I'M NOT MOVING FOR ANYTHING.

HAVE SOME RESPECT AND **LOOK** AT ME WHEN YOU SPEAK!

GO GET RESPECT FROM THE NEGATION! **THEY'RE** YOUR FAMILY NOW!

KAM**FIR**--

YOU'RE **DEAD** TO US, KOMPTIN! **STAY** THAT WAY!

WHOA! DID YOU **SEE** THAT?! **TRIPLE** BONUS!

ALL RIGHT, LITTLE BROTHER. YOU'VE GROWN UP ENOUGH NOW TO TAKE **RESPONSIBILITY** FOR YOUR DECISIONS.

SO UNDERSTAND **THIS:** IF YOU DON'T PUT MOTHER ON THE PHONE **RIGHT NOW...**

...I SWEAR BY HOLY CHARON THAT I WILL COME DOWN THERE IN PERSON...

...AND **FEED** YOU YOUR OWN **EYEBALLS.**

MOM...!

SO, KAMFIR **WAS** TELLING THE TRUTH...

HELLO, MOTHER.

"HELLO"--? IS THAT **ALL** YOU HAVE TO SAY FOR YOURSELF?

I KNOW YOU'RE PROBABLY WONDERING WHY I NEVER GOT IN TOUCH AFTER I **ENLISTED.**

EIGHT YEARS WITHOUT A WORD FROM ME, NOT EVEN WHEN **FATHER** DIED.

I'M SURE YOU FEEL YOU DESERVE AN **EXPLANATION...**

...BUT I REALLY **COULDN'T CARE LESS.**

THEN WHAT DO YOU **WANT** FROM ME?

I'M HERE TO PICK UP **GULLIT.**

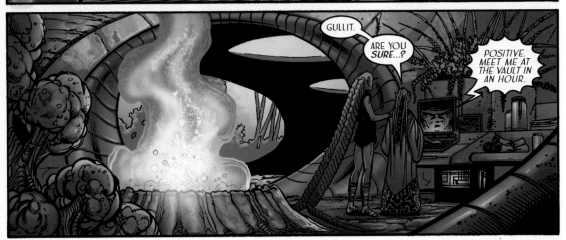

GULLIT.

ARE YOU **SURE**...?

POSITIVE. MEET ME AT THE VAULT IN AN HOUR.

OKAY, YOU'RE HEALED. READY TO TAKE ON THAT MONSTER?

DON'T LET GO, JAVI. PRETEND YOU'RE *STILL* HEALING ME.

BUT...

LOOK...I DON'T KNOW IF WE CAN *BEAT* HIM--! I'M...

JAVI, I'M *AFRAID*.

SCUTTLING...

...SCURRYING...

...VERMIN...

ALL OF YOU -- *STOP!*

Ah.

OUR ONLY HOPE IS TO HIT HIM ALL *TOGETHER!*

C'MON, EVINLEA!

BUT--

NOTHING *FANCY--*

WESTIN! GET TO THE *SHIP* AND START HER UP! TIME TO *SKY* OUTTA HERE!

WON'T THAT THING JUST *CRUNCH* US LIKE A CHUG-CAN ONCE WE'RE ALL INSIDE?

NOT IF HE'S DISTRACTED. ME AND EVINLEA CAN TAKE CARE OF *THAT!*

EVERYBODY GET TO THE *SHIP!* WE'RE DUSTING OFF *ASAP!*

GET HER OUT OF HARM'S WAY, MATUA! I'LL--

STIMULATING.

MY MOST STIMULATING ENCOUNTER IN A VERY, *VERY* LONG TIME.

GET YOUR FILTHY HANDS *OFF ME!*

LOOK OUT!

WRONG WAY, KAINE!

WHERE'S ZAIDA?

LORDS OF HALGEDAE... WHY TAKE *JAVI*... WHY *HIM*?

ZAIDA! HIT THE--

SHRANT

--DECK--!

...ZAIDA...

...MEMI...

MURDERER! COWARD! BABY KILLER!

SO...YOU'VE ACTUALLY COME TO *CARE* FOR THESE VERMIN...?

GET EVERYONE INTO THE SHIP AND *GO.* EVINLEA AND I WILL STAY BEHIND AND KEEP THE LAWBRINGER BUSY.

DOES... *SHE* KNOW YOU'RE VOLUNTEERING HER TO DIE...?

THAT THING'S *OBSESSED* WITH HER -- SHE'S DEAD ALREADY.

AAHHH -- WAHHHHH....!

Eh?

FINAL CHANCE TO *RECONSIDER.*

HROONK

I CAN *HANDLE* HIM, MOTHER. I'VE *CHANGED.*

⇒SIGH⇐

NOT REALLY. I *STILL* CAN'T TELL YOU A THING.

I JUST HOPE YOU *WARNED* YOUR MEN.

YEAH, YEAH...

WHRRR

K-CHNK

ZZZK

MEN...

...MEET *GULLIT.*

SIR...?

YOU MEAN WE DISOBEYED THE LAWBRINGER FOR *THAT* LAZY PILE OF HIDE?

NEVER SEEN A KALIMAN RETRIEVER, huh? *RELEASE* YOUR HOUNDS.

GYAOWWRRL!

HREENK*

HREEK*

SHREDDER--!

FALL BACK! FALL BACK!

GOOD DOG, GULLIT. YOU *REMEMBER* ME, RIGHT? YES... YES YOU *DO*...

WELL... AT LEAST IT WON'T BE ON *OUR* PLANET ANYMORE...

ARRR!

THE SENTENCE FOR HERESY IS--

WHUNG

NO, QZTR. THIS ONE STILL SERVES OUR PURPOSES.

TRIAL LOG: index entry
SUBJECT: human infant (ref--prison escape 001)

AGENDA: determine subject's
terminal threshold

IN THE NAME OF THE CREATOR, MAY YOU REST IN PEACE...

...QUOLZAG... ...PING...MIEJELL... AGLAREB...

...JAVI...

SORRY I COULDN'T COME UP WITH SOMETHING BETTER.

IT'LL HAVE TO DO, MATUA. YOU'RE THE CLOSEST WE HAVE TO A HOLY MAN.

DON'T GIVE UP HOPE. THE DARK ONE DIDN'T ACTUALLY *SLAY* YOUR CHILD. WE MAY YET *RESCUE* HIM.

HER. MEMI'S A HER.

...THANK YOU, UM...

IRESS.

IRESS.

IRESS...WHAT DO THEY *WANT* WITH MY *BABY*...?

I USED TO *WATCH* YOU BACK ON THE PRISON-WORLD. I ALWAYS *FELT* FOR YOU AND THAT POOR CHILD IN SUCH A HOSTILE ENVIRONMENT...

YOU'RE A REMARKABLE *MOTHER* TO HAVE KEPT HER ALIVE THIS LONG.

THAT'S *RICH*, CONSIDERING IT WAS ALL AN *ACCIDENT* IN THE FIRST PLACE...

"I WAS *ADOPTED*. WE LIVED MILES FROM OUR NEAREST NEIGHBOR.

"MY BIGGEST THRILL WAS THE ODD TRIP INTO TOWN WHEN I MIGHT ACTUALLY SEE A NEW FACE, OR GET NEWS FROM THE *CITY*.

"MY FOLKS WEREN'T *BAD* PEOPLE, BUT THEY WEREN'T VERY OPEN WITH THEIR FEELINGS, EITHER. THEY THOUGHT JOKES WERE IDLE CHATTER AND MUSIC WAS THE DEVIL'S WORK.

"I LOVED THEM, BUT I COULDN'T WAIT TO GET AWAY FROM THEM.

"THEN ONE DAY THE TRACTOR BROKE DOWN AND THE DEALERSHIP SENT OUT *A MAN*. HE STAYED WITH US FOR *TWO DAYS*.

"BY THEN HE'D *FIXED* THE TRACTOR...AND LEFT MY LIFE IN *SHREDS*..."

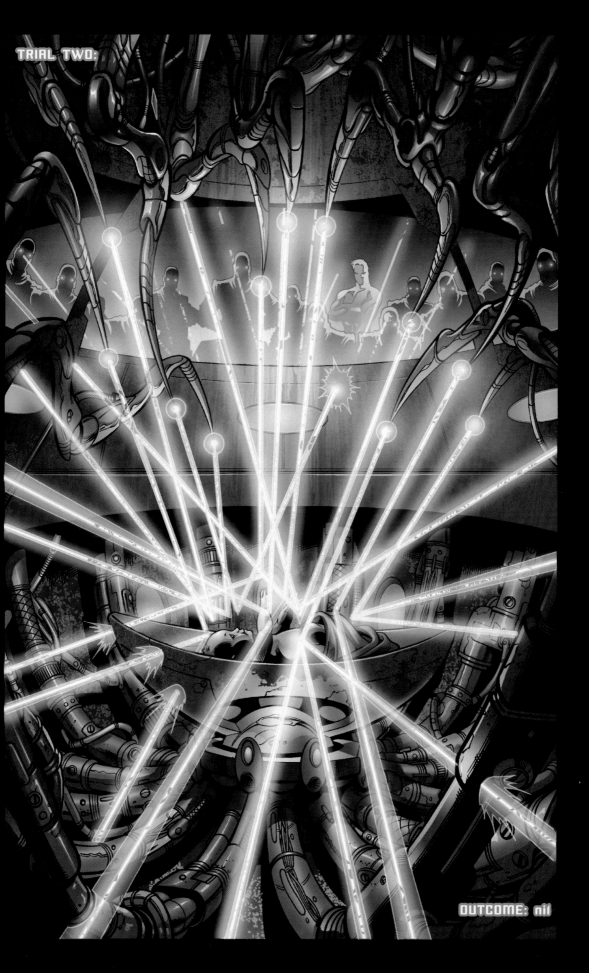

"HIS NAME WAS COBI. I HAD NEVER SEEN ANYTHING LIKE HIM."

"I NEVER EVEN QUESTIONED THAT HE'D *CALL* ME... AND *WRITE*...AND *COME BACK* FOR ME ONE DAY.

"OF COURSE, HE NEVER DID.

"A FEW MONTHS LATER, I COULD NO LONGER HIDE WHAT HAD *HAPPENED* DURING THOSE TWO DAYS. MY PARENTS FELT BETRAYED. THEY THREW ME OUT.

"I WENT TO LITA CITY, WHERE COBI SAID HE LIVED, BUT HE WASN'T *LISTED* IN THE COMMBOOK.

"BY THE TIME I FIGURED OUT THAT FINDING ONE PERSON IN A CITY OF THREE MILLION IS PRETTY NEAR IMPOSSIBLE, ALL MY HOPES HAD BEEN *CRUSHED*..."

"SO I GOT A JOB, RENTED A SHOEBOX APARTMENT, AND SPENT MY DAYS WONDERING WHY THE ONLY GOOD THING THAT EVER HAPPENED TO ME HAD GONE SO WRONG.

"I DIDN'T KNOW WHO I WAS, OR WHO I WANTED TO BE. I DIDN'T HAVE A CLUE WHY GOD EVER WASTED A LIFE ON *ME*. AND I *BLAMED* THE LIFE THAT WAS GROWING *WITHIN* ME.

"AND THEN ONE MORNING I WOKE UP IN *THIS* UNIVERSE WITH NO IDEA HOW I GOT HERE. I ONLY KNEW THAT MY PASSAGE HAD BROUGHT ON THE *BIRTH*.

"IT WAS THE FINAL INDIGNITY. I *HATED* THAT CHILD--

"--RIGHT UP UNTIL I FIRST SAW HER *FACE*:

"MY EYES AND NOSE, COBI'S MOUTH AND JAW, ALL BLENDED INTO ONE *PERFECT* LITTLE PACKAGE.

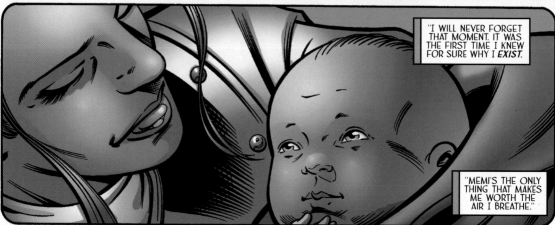

"I WILL NEVER FORGET THAT MOMENT. IT WAS THE FIRST TIME I KNEW FOR SURE WHY I *EXIST*.

"MEMI'S THE ONLY THING THAT MAKES ME WORTH THE AIR I BREATHE."

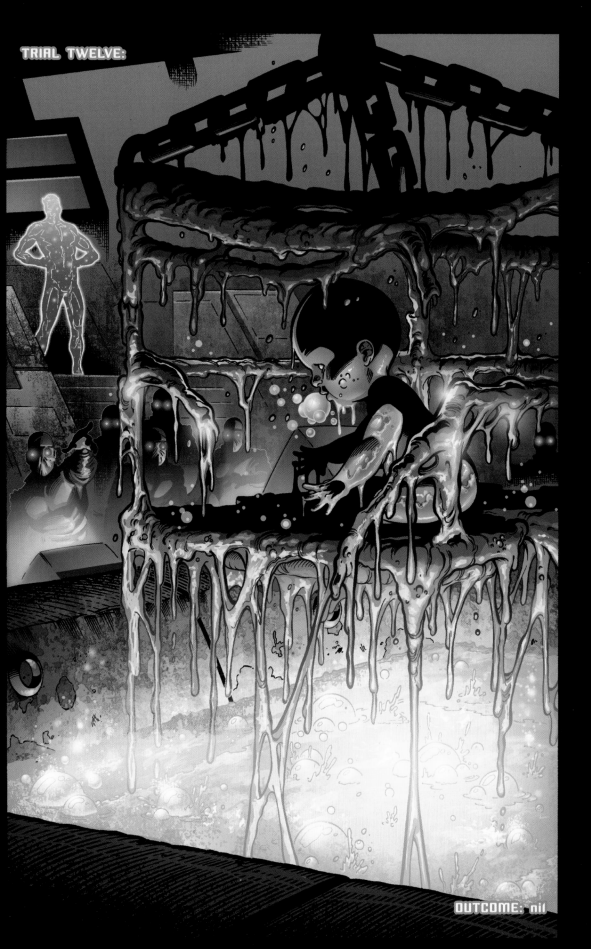

OUTCOME: nil

OUTCOME: nil

OUTCOME: nil

...SO IF WHAT YOU'RE TELLING ME ABOUT YOUR SIGIL IS ACCURATE, THEN THIS RESCUE ALL COMES DOWN TO *RECON*...

...STARTING WITH THE LAWBRINGER'S *LOCATION.*

UNFORTUNATELY, THE ONLY ONES WITH THAT KIND OF INTEL ARE GOING TO BE NEGATION *TOP BRASS*...

...OR *ANOTHER* LAWBRINGER.

I'D RATHER TAKE MY CHANCES WITH *SANE* KILLERS.

YOU AND ME, BOTH.

"*FLUXOR* MIGHT KNOW WHICH NEGATION GENERALS ARE CLOSEST TO THE TOP.

"HE'S *NATIVE* TO NEGATION SPACE. DID YOUR GROUP ENCOUNTER ANY LOCALS, OR PICK UP A *GUIDE?*"

"YEAH. THE CURLY-HAIRED ONE THE LAWBRINGER *SKEWERED* ON HIS FINGERTIPS."

"SO THEN CAPTAIN FLUXOR IS OUR *BEST* SOURCE OF INTEL...?

"BOHICA."

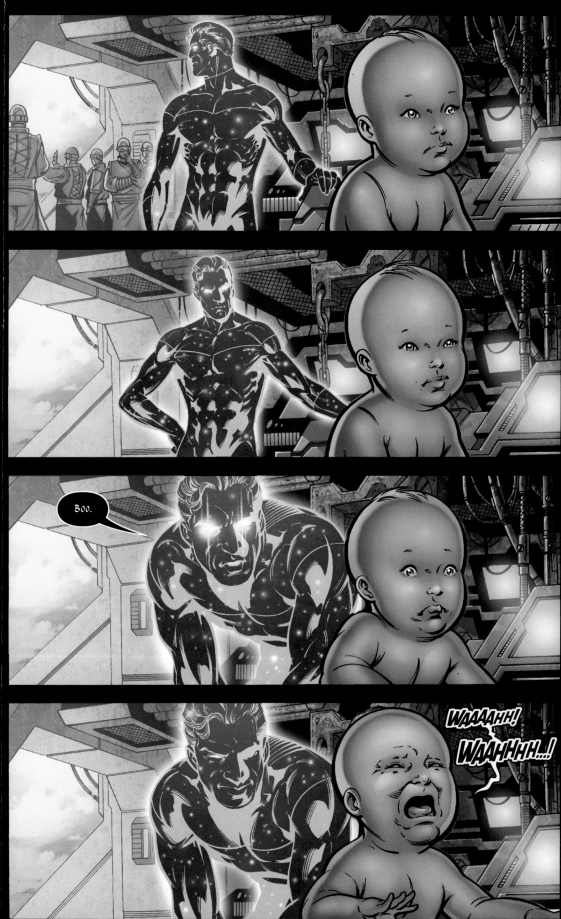

TODAY'S COMMCAST IS DEVOTED TO OUR MOST *VENERATED* MILITARY LEADER -- A MAN WHO WAS *INSTRUMENTAL* IN CONQUERING THIS GALAXY FOR THE GREATER GLORY OF *CHARON*, BLESSED BE HIS NAME...

GREATEST WAR HERO IN HISTORY? SHORT'A THE EMPEROR HIMSELF? THAT'S EASY: GENERAL MURQUADE.

HEY, IS HE GONNA SEE THIS?

We used to be the richest planet in the sector until *he* crashed the **moon** down on us for cheating the tithe.

That was five hundred **annos** ago. Folks still don't repeat his **name** around here.

HE GAVE US A CHANCE TO *SURRENDER*, AND *WE DID*. THE OTHER CITY-STATES CHOSE TO FIGHT.

THEY'RE ALL GONE NOW...

EVERY YEAR WE GET FLOODED WITH REQUESTS FOR *TRANSFERS* INTO THE GENERAL'S BATTLE GROUP. TELL YOU *THIS*: THEY'RE NOT GETTING *MY* SLOT.

WE REGRET THAT GENERAL MURQUADE WAS UNAVAILABLE FOR AN INTERVIEW, AS BATTLE GROUP *CLARION* DEPLOYED TO THE RAMPHO SYSTEM TO HUNT SOME *TROUBLEMAKERS* WHO WILL SOON BE VERY, VERY *SORRY*...

IN FACT, GENERAL, THEY WALKED INTO OUR OUTPOST ON DAGRAX REQUESTING TO SURRENDER TO *YOU* PERSONALLY.

AND WHAT MAKES THEM THINK THEY CAN WASTE *MY* TIME...

WAIT A MINUTE. THESE TWO LOOK *FAMILIAR*. THERE WAS A *PRISON ESCAPE* NEAR THE PERIPHERY A FEW WEEKS AGO....

GOOD WORK, COLONEL.

YES, SIR. *ORDERS?*

PAFF

INFORM THE BRIG CASTELLAN THAT I'LL BE CONDUCTING THIS INTERROGATION *MYSELF.*

IN THE MEANTIME, KEEP THE BATTLE GROUP SEARCHING FOR OUR *PRIME OBJECTIVE.* MIND-LINK ME THE INSTANT A SEARCH TEAM REPORTS *CONTACT...*

GENERAL! THIS IS A RARE HONOR! ALLOW ME TO --

JUST TAKE ME TO THEM, CASTELLAN.

OF COURSE, SIR. RIGHT THIS WAY...

"NOT IN TEN MILLENNIA HAVE I FACED SUCH A MYSTERY..."

"ORANGE EYES AND NATURAL PSYCHIC BARRIERS... JUST LIKE YOURS --"

-- BUT *UNLIKE* YOU, SHE IS NOT FROM *ATLANTIS.*

IN FACT, SHE ISN'T EVEN FROM *EARTH.*

YOU LIKE TO SEE ME BAFFLED, DON'T YOU?

MY UNCERTAINTY, MY *TORMENT* IS YOUR SOLE COMFORT.

ENJOY IT WHILE YOU *CAN.* ONCE MURQUADE ROUNDS UP THE REST OF YOUR COHORTS, ONE OF *THEM* IS SURE TO TALK, AND THEN YOUR STAY HERE WILL COME TO AN *END.*

I STILL CAN'T BELIEVE I WAS STUPID ENOUGH TO ACTUALLY *AGREE* TO THIS PLAN!

I MEAN, THERE'S *STILL* NO WORD FROM HER! WHAT IF OUR CLOAKING FIELD IS KEEPING HER FROM GETTING THROUGH TO US?

I'M PRETTY SURE THE *STEALTH SPHERE* ONLY BLOCKS MECHANICAL SENSORS.

ONCE SHE FINDS OUT WHERE YOUR BABY IS, HER TELEPATHIC CALL SHOULD GET THROUGH JUST FINE...

...I *THINK*.

AND WHAT IF SHE JUST SOLD US OUT AND CUT HER *OWN* DEAL WITH THE NEGATION?

THAT'S EXACTLY WHAT THEY'D EXPECT FROM HER, WHICH IS WHY SHE'S THE BEST CHOICE TO *INFILTRATE* THEM.

I KNOW IT DOESN'T FEEL RIGHT, *TRUSTING* EVINLEA, BUT THIS IS THE *SMARTEST* THING WE COULD DO.

BELIEVE ME, I'VE BEEN WORKING ON HER SINCE DAY ONE. SHE'S *READY* FOR US TO SHOW SOME *FAITH* IN HER.

MISTER KAINE, I KNOW I'D BE *DEAD* BY NOW IF NOT FOR YOU, BUT YOU'RE STAKING MY DAUGHTER'S *LIFE* ON YOUR ABILITY TO READ PEOPLE.

NO...

...I'M STAKING *ALL* OUR LIVES ON IT.

KAINE. A WORD...

ALL RIGHT, SO YOU CAN READ PEOPLE. WELL, EVINLEA'S *NOT* A PERSON. SHE'S A ZILLION YEAR-OLD GODDESS WHOSE ONLY PURPOSE IS TO PROVIDE FOR *HERSELF*.

I THINK SHE'LL *VERY* LIKELY DOUBLE-CROSS US.

WHY DO YOU THINK I SENT *IRESS* WITH HER?

YOU JUST BE READY WHEN *YOUR* TURN COMES...

STOP! YOU'RE *KILLING* ME!

I *MEAN* IT: ONE MORE COURSE, AND I SHALL SIMPLY DROP DEAD WITH DELIGHT!

YOUR PRAISE *HONORS* US, LADY EVINLEA. WOULD THAT YOUR COMPANION WERE *HALF* AS ENTHUSIASTIC.

I... I'M SORRY, I DON'T MEAN TO SEEM *UNGRATEFUL*, IT'S JUST...

I CAN'T ENJOY MYSELF WHEN I KNOW THAT POOR *BABY* IS OUT THERE SOMEWHERE *SUFFERING*...

YOU DIDN'T MENTION HAVING A CHILD...

SHE REFERS TO ONE OF OUR FORMER COMPANIONS WHOSE INFANT DAUGHTER WAS *STOLEN* BY A NEGATION OPERATIVE --

-- A CREATURE CALLING ITSELF *LAWBRINGER QZTR.*

Ah, QZTR...

IGNORE HER. SHE IS ONLY *HALF* DESCENDED FROM MY PEOPLE, AND LACKS OUR USUAL *WISDOM* AND *PATIENCE*.

AS FOR YOUR ENTERING MY MIND, I *DO* ANTICIPATE SUCH FUTURE...*INTIMACY* BETWEEN US, MY GENERAL.

BUT REMEMBER: I CAME HERE WILLINGLY. LET'S *NOT RUSH* A FRUITFUL RELATIONSHIP.

DAMN YOU, EVINLEA, THIS *WASN'T* THE PLAN...

PLAN...?

KAINE AND THE OTHERS BELIEVE I SURRENDERED TO YOU AS A *RUSE* TO FIND OUT *WHERE* THE LAW-BRINGER TOOK THE CHILD.

AND...?

I COULDN'T CARE LESS ABOUT THE MEWLING LITTLE BRAT. I'M HERE TO STRIKE WHATEVER *BARGAIN* WILL RETURN ME *HOME* TO FAIR ELYSIA.

NO!

YES...WE *CAN* COME TO TERMS...

⇒MFF!⇐

EVINLEA, PLEASE, BEFORE IT'S TOO LATE...

GET OVER IT, IRESS.

SIT-REP?

STILL NO CONFIRMED SIGHTINGS OF OUR *QUARRY*, BUT WE'VE LOST SEARCH TEAM SEVEN'S COMM-SIGNAL.

LAST POSITION?

NEAR PLANET FOUR.

SEND THE *AEGIS* AND A FIGHTER ESCORT TO FIND THEM. AND OPEN A COMMLINK TO THE *THRONEWORLD*. I WOULD SPEAK WITH THE *LOGOS*.

AYE, SIR.

BRIDGE CREW! AVERT YOUR GAZE FOR CONTACT WITH THE *EMPEROR!*

COMMLINK ESTABLISHED. ACTIVATING MAIN SCREEN...

FORGIVE THE INTRUSION, LORD, BUT I BELIEVE I HAVE SOMETHING OF *INTEREST* TO YOU.

MURQUADE! HAVE YOU FOUND THEM YE--

WELL, WELL.

PRISONER *EVINLEA?*

YES, LORD. SHE TURNED HERSELF IN. SHE'LL LEAD US TO THE *OTHER* ESCAPEES IN EXCHANGE FOR PASSAGE BACK TO HER UNIVERSE.

AS FOR OUR PRIME OBJECTIVE, WE HAVE SOME LEADS, BUT NOTHING CONCRETE.

CONTINUE THE SEARCH. RIGHT NOW, I AM *MORE* INTERESTED IN FINDING THE MOTHER OF THIS *CHILD.* SHE IS AMONG EVINLEA'S FORMER COMRADES.

SHE'S AS GOOD AS YOURS, LORD, BUT...

...HOW COULD SHE POSSIBLY MERIT *YOUR* ATTENTION?

KAINE! THE CHILD IS ON THE NEGATION *THRONE-WORLD!*

DRAKE-- WE'RE ON THE BRIDGE OF THE *FLAGSHIP!* HURRY!

IT'S ALL UP TO *YOU* NOW. GOOD LUCK.

LUCK'S GOT *NOTHING* TO DO WITH IT...

GENERAL! YOUR INFORMANT JUST TRANSMITTED A TELEPATHIC CALL.

YES, LORD. I HEARD IT, TOO.

TACTICAL! SENSOR-LASH EVERYTHING WITHIN FIVE MEGA-KLIKS. THEY'LL BE IN STEALTH MODE, BUT MAYBE WE CAN FLUSH THEM OUT.

AYE, SIR!

CONTACT ME WHEN YOU HAVE THEM IN CUSTODY.

OF COURSE, LORD. IF YOU'LL PLEASE PARDON ME...

EEEE EEEE EEEF

THEY'VE FOUND US!

WE GOTTA GET OUT OF HERE!

NEGATIVE, WESTIN. HOLD POSITION. IF WHAT DRAKE TOLD ME IS TRUE, HE'LL BE BACK HERE WITH EVINLEA AND IRESS IN ABOUT TEN MINUTES.

WHAT EXACTLY DID HE SAY?

HE TOLD ME WHAT HIS SIGIL DOES...

"IT TURNS OUT THOSE RED AND YELLOW TATTOOS JUST MAKE YOU *MORE* OF WHAT YOU ALREADY *ARE*.

"*JAVI* WAS A *DOCTOR*. HIS SIGIL LET HIM *HEAL* THOSE HE TOUCHED.

"*WESTIN* WAS A CROOK. *HIS* SIGIL LETS HIM OPERATE ANY TECHNOLOGY-- THE BETTER TO *STEAL* IT.

"*DRAKE* WAS A *PIRATE* IN MY OWN HOME SYSTEM, EVEN BEFORE HE GOT HIS SIGIL. AND PIRACY IS ALL ABOUT *ACQUISITION*.

"AS FOR *DRAKE*...

"HE CLAIMS *HIS* SIGIL GIVES HIM *ANY* ABILITY HE *NEEDS* TO TAKE WHATEVER HE *WANTS*.

"THINK ABOUT IT...

"...SO LONG AS HE HAS A SPECIFIC TARGET AND HE KNOWS ITS *LOCATION*, NOTHING CAN KEEP HIM FROM *TAKING* IT.

"HANDY TALENT FOR A RAID...OR AN *EXTRACTION*."

SIR, A SMALL, TORPEDO-SIZED OBJECT INCOMING. IT'S MADE SEVERAL COURSE CORRECTIONS.

BUT, IT'S NOT PUTTING OUT ANY THRUSTER SIGNATURE.

YOU'RE IN TROUBLE NOW.

GENERAL! EMERGENCY TRANSMISSION FROM THE *AEGIS!*

WHAT *NOW?!*

GENERAL MURQUADE! ⇒SKZZ⇐ WE'VE BEEN *BOARDED!* SITUATION ⇒SKZZ⇐ DETERIORATING!

SEND REINFORCEMENTS! ⇒SKZZZ⇐

DON'T *BOTHER,* GENERAL! ⇒SKZZ⇐ WE'LL COME TO YOU!

COLONEL, REGROUP OUR ASSETS!

SOUND THE *RED ALERT* -- WE'VE MADE CONTACT WITH THE *AUSTRALIANS*!

THE WHO...?

DRAKE? ARE YOU *IN* YET?

ALMOST. JUST CLEARING A PATH.

WHAT IN THE--?

SOMETHING WRONG?

NOT SURE...

DRAKE! CAN YOU STILL HEAR ME?!

WHO *ARE* THESE GUYS?

NO IDEA. THEY JUST SWOOPED IN OUT OF *NOWHERE.*

WHERE'S *EVINLEA* AND *IRESS?*

ON THE COMMAND SHIP'S *BRIDGE*... JUST BEFORE IT *EXPLODED.* IF THEY DIDN'T GET OUT IN TIME...

WE'LL HAVE TO HOPE FOR THE BEST...

...RIGHT NOW, I NEED YOU TO FIND WHOEVER'S *LEADING* THESE NEW PEOPLE AND BRING HIM TO *ME!*

"MY FIRST CLUE YOU'D NEVER TAKE HIM WAS THE FACT THAT THERE WAS NO PLAN, NO *DISCIPLINE* TO YOUR ATTACK.

"IT WAS JUST A *FREE-FOR-ALL:* TEN EGOS, ALL TRYING TO TAKE THEIR BEST SHOT.

"EVEN *DOGS* ARE SMARTER ABOUT HUNTING IN PACKS.

"MY SECOND CLUE WAS HOW THE NEGATION GENERAL CAREFULLY CONTROLLED THE *TERRAIN* OF BATTLE.

"BY KEEPING CLOSE TO THE DECK, HE CUT IN *HALF* THE DIRECTIONS FROM WHICH YOU COULD ATTACK HIM.

"*YOUR* PEOPLE FOUGHT LIKE CIVILIANS. *HE* FOUGHT LIKE MY HAND-TO-HAND INSTRUCTOR FROM BOOT CAMP, GUNNY BLANCHARD..."

"I CAN STILL SEE GUNNY LAUGHING AS HE'D WHIP TEN RECRUITS AT A TIME...

"...HE ALWAYS SAID, 'TEN UNFRIENDLIES, OR TEN THOUSAND, IT MAKES NO DIFFERENCE: JUST WORRY ABOUT THE *ONE* YOU'RE KILLING *NOW.*'

"ANYHOW, MY POINT IS THAT YOU NEED A *PLAN OF ATTACK*, WHICH IS WHY I ASKED DRAKE TO BRING YOU HERE...

"...AND I'M GLAD HE MANAGED TO DO IT BEFORE YOU GOT YOURSELF *KILLED* TAKING ON THAT GENERAL..."

...SEE, I THINK WE'RE ON THE *SAME SIDE*, AND I DON'T WANT YOU THROWING YOUR LIVES AWAY.

MY NAME'S *OBREGON KAINE.* WHAT'S YOURS?

THE CLARION IS ENTERING THE PLANET'S ATMOSPHERE. ALL HANDS ABANDON SHIP!

HURRY UP, HALF-BLOOD--

--WE'LL BE TAKING A DIFFERENT EXIT THAN THE REST OF THESE DAMNED FOOLS.

YOU! TURN RIGHT AROUND! UNAUTHORIZED PERSONNEL ARE--

I TRUST THIS FACILITY IS THE ONE YOUR GENERAL MENTIONED--THE DEVICE YOU EMPLOY TO REACH THE OTHER UNIVERSE. MY UNIVERSE.

ACTIVATE THE GATEWAY NOW, IF YOU WISH TO KEEP A HEAD ON YOUR SHOULDERS.

IF WE HIT THE ATMOSPHERE WITH THE GATE STILL ACTIVE--

AS LONG AS I AM ALREADY THROUGH IT, IT MAKES NO DIFFERENCE WHAT HAPPENS HERE.

IT **WORKED**, DRAKE. WE KILLED THE BEAST, BUT HE TOOK A DOZEN OF MY PEOPLE WITH HIM.

WE MUST HURRY NOW-- THE SHIP IS FALLING, AND YOUR LEADER SAID YOU HAD TO RETRIEVE A PAIR OF **YOUR** PEOPLE ON BOARD...

MY **LEADER,** huh...? GOTTA HAVE A **TALK** WHEN THIS IS OVER...

FWASH

THERE. **YOUR** UNIVERSE.

ALTWAAL'S BLESSED EYES...

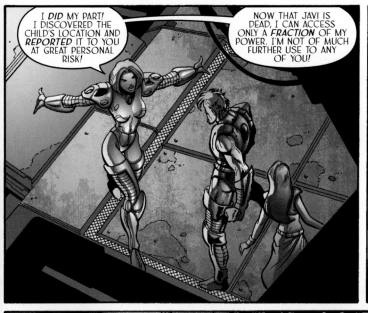

I *DID* MY PART! I DISCOVERED THE CHILD'S LOCATION AND *REPORTED* IT TO YOU AT GREAT PERSONAL RISK!

NOW THAT JAVI IS DEAD, I CAN ACCESS ONLY A *FRACTION* OF MY POWER. I'M NOT OF MUCH FURTHER USE TO ANY OF YOU!

FARE THEE WELL WITH THE RESCUE, AND MAY YOU ALL ONE DAY RETURN HOME AS *I* SHALL.

YOU UNBELIEVABLY SELFISH--

SPUT-SPUT--

--COW!

SPuTHOOM

LET'S ALL GET OFF THIS STINKING SHIP BEFORE IT'S TOO LATE.

SIR, I JUST RELINKED WITH THE COMMWEB. WE HAVE AN UPDATE CONCERNING THE *FUGITIVES*.

IT SAYS THAT PRISONERS EVINLEA AND IRESS RETURNED *THEMSELVES* TO CUSTODY, AND WERE TURNED OVER TO BATTLE GROUP *CLARION*.

GENERAL MURQUADE'S TASK FORCE.

MAYBE KAINE COULDN'T BEND THEM TO HIS WILL. THEY ARE IMMORTALS AFTER ALL.

OR MAYBE...

HAIL THE *CLARION*.

ONE MOMENT...

SIR! BATTLE GROUP *CLARION* IS *RETREATING* FROM THE RAMPHO SYSTEM!

THEY'RE REPORTING A LOSS OF TWO ESCORTS AND THE COMMAND SHIP--AND THE GENERAL HIMSELF IS *DEAD*!

WARP TO RAMPHO IMMEDIATELY!

GENERAL KRYZZOR'S *ORDERS* WERE--

LET HIM PULL OUT *HIS* SHIPS. *WE* WORK FOR THE LAWBRINGER NOW, AND I SAY WE GO IN.

PRISONER *KAINE* IS BEHIND THIS SOMEHOW, I *KNOW* IT! SENDING THOSE TWO IN TO "SURRENDER" IS JUST THE SORT OF DEVIOUS *TRICK* HE'S GOOD AT.

OKAY...A MILLION TONS OF RUNAWAY STARSHIP MIGHT MAKE FOR A NICE DIVERSION, BUT HOW WILL WE REPROGRAM THE JUMP-GATE?

WESTIN...?

YEAH, YEAH, I'M WORKING ON IT.

DON'T KNOW HOW, BUT HIS *SIGIL* LETS HIM WORK ANY TECHNOLOGY WE'VE FOUND. WITH LUCK, THE *SHIP'S COMPUTER* WILL GIVE UP THE CODES.

LOOK, I HELPED YOU RAISE THIS SHIP BECAUSE YOU HELPED US EARLIER. BUT WHY WOULD I LEAD MY PEOPLE RIGHT INTO THE *TEETH* OF MY ENEMY?

YOU'RE RIGHT--IT'S NOT YOUR FIGHT. WE'RE DOING THIS TO SAVE A *CHILD* HELD BY THE EMPEROR.

WHY WERE *YOU* FIGHTING THE NEGATION?

THEY'VE *HUNTED* US EVER SINCE WE CAME HERE FROM ANOTHER UNIVERSE, FROM A PLANET CALLED EARTH.

THE TRANSITION TO THIS PLACE GAVE US THE POWER YOU NOW SEE. IT ALSO DROVE US TEMPORARILY *INSANE.*

ANOTHER WHO CROSSED OVER WITH US--ONE WHO ALREADY POSSESSED GREAT POWER AND WISDOM--HELPED *QUELL* OUR MADNESS AND HARNESS OUR NEW POWER.

HIS NAME IS *GAMMID.* WE OWE HIM *EVERYTHING.*

THIS GAMMID, DID HE HAVE *WHITE HAIR?* AND AN *ORANGE MARK*--

ON HIS CHEST! *YES!* HAVE YOU *SEEN* HIM?

THEN PERHAPS OUR GOALS *DO* COINCIDE...

GOD KNOWS WE NEED ALL THE HELP WE CAN *GET.*

WESTIN, FLUXOR, SET IT UP! I'M GONNA GRAB SOME *SHUTEYE.* WAKE ME UP WHEN WE'RE READY TO HIT THE GATE.

HE IS HELD CAPTIVE ON THE THRONEWORLD, ALONGSIDE THE CHILD.

HEY! WAKE UP!

YOU'RE HAVING A *NIGHTMARE!*

HURRY, WE'RE COMING UP ON THE GATE.

HUH...? FEELS LIKE I JUST CLOSED MY EYES...

WESTIN MANAGED TO GET THE *CODES?*

IN LESS THAN TEN MINUTES. HE FOUND A MAP OF THE THRONEWORLD, TOO!

THEN OUR NEW FRIENDS ROUNDED UP THE WRECKED SHIPS AND *THREW* THE WHOLE MESS AT THE JUMP-GATE.

ABOUT TIME I DREAMED UP A FEW THINGS GOING OUR WAY, ISN'T IT?

Ah... RIGHT. THANKS, CORRIN.

GOOD, YOU'RE FINALLY HERE, KAINE. WE'VE JUST PASSED THROUGH THE GATE. THRONEWORLD DEAD AHEAD.

ALREADY?!

IT'S OKAY. LOCAL PERIMETER FORCES ARE CONVERGING ON THE BIG SHIP. NO ONE'S NOTICED *US.*

LET'S GIVE SAMAKAR'S PEOPLE TIME TO MAKE THE FRONTAL ASSAULT *CONVINCING.*

HARD TO STARBOARD, THEN ALL-STOP.

DONE AND DONE.

HANG ON... SOMETHING JUST CAME THROUGH THE GATE *BEHIND* US...

Know Your
Negation

War is never a simple affair, but when it involves one hundred total strangers abducted from one universe and stranded in another, it can get downright complicated. Every month, CrossGen's sci-fi thriller NEGATION serves up wild new locales and bizarre characters, each a distinct and vital part of our great tapestry of cosmic combat. For those who want a better sense of the big picture, we present this guide to the heroes of our trans-galactic epic.

THE "BRIGHT UNIVERSE"

Obregon Kaine and his fellow fugitives hail from scores of different worlds in the CrossGen Universe, which their Negation enemies sometimes refer to as the "Bright Universe." This cosmos, in which every other series in the CrossGen Comics line is set, is home to a wide variety of life forms and races.

Humans are by far the most prevalent intelligent species in the CrossGen Universe. Originating on planet Earth, humankind now inhabits a plethora of worlds with names like Kazrath, Ciress, Larrinaga, and Demetria. Some humans in NEGATION were abducted from interstellar communities comprising multiple worlds. Others amongst the Negation captives were not previously aware that there were any planets out there populated by humans.

Less well known is Earth's *original* dominant species — the mighty **Atlanteans** — an older human race who actually preceded our species on Earth by millions of years. Atlanteans possess great psionic powers, allowing them to perform a multitude of superhuman feats.

Other sentient humanoids, such as the fierce **Saurians** of planet Tcharun and the godlike **First** of planet Elysia, are forces to be reckoned with in distant corners of the Bright Universe.

It is from this wide assortment of worlds and species that the Negation randomly abducted test subjects and placed them on a Prison World at the edge of the Negation Universe. Those who escaped along with Kaine are truly lost in a strange, chaotic cosmos.

THE FUGITIVES

Aglareb (troll/deceased) was a warrior from the feudal world of Quin. He was slain by Lawbringer Qztr on planet Vassa.

Calyx (human) is from the relatively primitive world of Demetria. She retains her weasel-like pet, Foonie, although neither of them offers much in a battle since both Calyx and Foonie lack any special powers or abilities.

Corrin (Atlantean) believes she is still asleep in a stasis pod in her home, the city-state of Atlantis, and that all the bizarre things she's encountered in Negation Space are just part of one big, vivid dream. This may be her mind's defense mechanism when faced with such horrors, but soon Corrin must awaken and use her telekinetic powers to help the fugitives fight their guerilla struggle against the Negation.

Evinlea (a First) is as self-centered as she is powerful. Her godlike powers have made her indispensable to the team, but her uncertain loyalties make her just as big a threat to her companions.

Exor (Kremmin/deceased) was the First Officer aboard Captain Fluxor's vessel, the *Outreach*. Exor was slain, along with the other remnants of the kremmin crew, while held prisoner on planet Senkiem.

Fluxor (Kremmin) is a native of Negation Space whose species was wiped out by the Negation Empire. Formerly a captain aboard a vessel of science and exploration, Fluxor now serves as a guide and advisor to the fugitives.

Gammid (Atlantean) was one of a group of Atlanteans who awoke on Earth to battle Negation incursions on that planet. Gammid crossed over to Negation Space with a group of humans from Australia and has fought for his life ever since. The strange orange sigil on Gammid's chest allows his electromagnetic powers to operate smoothly despite the disruptive effect Negation Space has on everyone else's powers. His impact on Kaine's team… and on Kaine's leadership position, has yet to be determined.

Harvey (human/deceased) was a citizen of the Victorian-era world of Arcadia. Little was known of him before he met his demise at the hands of Lawbringer Qztr on planet Vassa.

Iress (half human/half First) is a so-called half-blood from Elysia, homeworld of the First. Though she is half human, Iress possesses many of the vast powers that the godlike First enjoy. Naturally meek, Iress has demurred to Evinlea's will and charisma, but Evinlea's betrayals have turned Iress against her.

Javi (human/deceased) was a Sigil-Bearer with the ability to increase the natural energies in whomever he touched. This meant that he could speed a person's natural healing abilities. He could also increase the superhuman abilities of others — a fact which Evinlea took great advantage of when she made Javi her paramour. Unfortunately, Javi was slain by Lawbringer Qztr on planet Vassa.

Lizard Lady (Saurian) is a warrior from a reptilian race capable of absorbing useful genetic traits from any species it consumes. While on the icy planet Senkiem, Lizard Lady absorbed gills, claws and coloration from the amphibious natives. Although her true name is Khlystek, she is known simply as the Lizard Lady to the other fugitives.

Matua (human) is a wizard from the magical world of Ciress. A member of the Djinn Guild, he uses his mystic spells to defend his comrades.

Mercer Drake (human) was a space pirate in the same solar system that Kaine hails from. Drake's sigil grants him a multitude of abilities. Essentially, if there is some item Drake desires and he knows its location, his sigil gives him any power (strength, flight, intangibility, etc.) necessary to capture it, making Drake the most formidable Sigil-Bearer in the group — and a bit of a loose cannon.

Miejell (species unknown/deceased) was a native of Negation Space who served as a guide for Mercer Drake's band of escapees before they reunited with Kaine's group. She was slain by Lawbringer Qztr on planet Vassa.

Harvey

Iress

Javi

Lizard Lady

Matua

Mercer Drake

Miejell

Monchito (species unknown) is an alien with limited language skills and a seemingly limitless appetite. Despite his great agility, Monchito has shown little flair for combat.

Obregon Kaine (human) leads our intrepid band of escaped prisoners. His military experience and guile earn him the respect of his companions and keep many of them alive through their odyssey. Unlike many of those he leads, Kaine has no special powers or abilities beyond his courage, cunning and indomitable spirit.

Ping Lam Wu (human/deceased) was a martial artist from the planet Han-Jin. He revealed next to nothing about himself before being killed by Lawbringer Qztr.

Rat-Boy (Lesser Races/deceased) was a genetic hybrid from the techno-medieval world of Avalon. He was killed by Komptin prior to the escape from the Negation prison world.

Quolzag (species unknown/deceased) was an alien abducted from the Bright Universe. Little was known of him when he was slain by Lawbringer Qztr on planet Vassa.

Samakar (human) is the leader of the band of Australians who crossed over to Negation Space with Gammid. They thought they were undergoing "transition" — a process meant to ascend humans and Atlanteans to a higher, more powerful state of being. Instead, the transition cast Samakar's people into Negation Space even as it imbued them with great, yet unstable power. Only Gammid's power-stabilizing sigil saved the supercharged Australians from themselves.

Shassa (human) was a law enforcement officer on her homeworld. Her sigil allows her to borrow power from whomever she battles, allowing her to fight as an equal against any foe she faces. Shassa is loyal to Kaine.

Thalia (species unknown/deceased) was an alien who served as an empowered underling to one of the First back on her homeworld. She was killed in the escape from the Negation prison world.

Thustra (species unknown) is a humanoid of undetermined origin who travels with the fugitives, though she has thus far offered little contribution to their war against the Negation.

Thustra

Westin (human) was a scam artist and master scrounger before he was abducted by the Negation. The sigil in his right eye gives Westin the ability to operate any technology he encounters, though precisely how this ability works has yet to be explained. Westin is a charming rouge, but also an opportunist whose true loyalty lies only with himself.

Westin

Zaida & Memi (species unknown) are a mother and child who befriended Kaine early on in their captivity. While they appear to be ordinary humans, both have displayed an unnatural ability to withstand deadly forces, raising whispered questions from the rest of the fugitives.

Zaida

"NEGATION SPACE"

The universe that is ruled by the Negation Empire is sometimes referred to as the **Negation Universe** or **Negation Space.** It is every bit as vast as the CrossGen Universe, and it is caught in the iron grip of its godlike emperor, Charon. Negation Space is patrolled by the Negation's mighty space fleet. Its military fills its ranks with recruits from the many, many worlds under its domination, but the spine of this military force is the so-called **"Core Negation."** These humanoid soldiers are identified by the areas of their heads marked by a patch of energy shaped like the Negation symbol. The least powerful of the Core Negation are the **Soldiers** with one small marking over one of their eyes. Next up on the hierarchy are the **Officers**, who have an energy swath across both eyes. At the top of the command structure are the **Generals**, whose energy swaths obscure the entire top half of their heads. Since aliens native to Negation Space are encouraged to join the military, they may climb up to the status of officer, or even general. But they will never have the link to Charon that the Core Negation soldiers have. Additionally, there are special

Negation Space

Prison World

Throneworld

Senkiem

Kalima

Vassa

Periphery

Imperial Guard troops on the Throneworld who protect the Emperor himself. Finally, there are the **Lawbringers** — artificial beings created directly from Charon's own energies. Lawbringers function as independent adjudicators with power and authority comparable to the most powerful Generals in the fleet. They are notoriously cruel and capricious, and seldom work alongside regular Negation troops.

The origins of the Negation are obscured by a hundred centuries of history. It is known that Charon, Appolyon and the Core Negation all arrived in Negation Space ten thousand years ago. Driven mad by the journey from his point of origin, Charon eventually spewed out the insane portions of his own psyche, which took on a life of their own as his Lawbringers. Charon swiftly banished his rival Appolyon to a far off corner of reality, then began building his military around the Lawbringers and his faithful followers, the Core Negation. It was Charon who dubbed the empire "Negation," though his reason for doing so has yet to be revealed.

Thus far, we've seen several key locations in Negation Space, starting with the **Prison World** upon which Kaine and the fugitives were originally incarcerated. An even more important planet is the **Throneworld**, a huge construct made from several smaller planets pushed together. This is the seat of Charon's empire. Lesser Negation worlds visited by the fugitives include the frigid world **Senkiem,** Komptin's homeworld **Kalima,** the abandoned junkworld known as **Vassa**, and planet **Rampho,** above which General Murquade's fleet engaged Samakar's super-powered Australians. Other noteworthy sights include the **Periphery** of the Negation Universe, the now-defunct federation of worlds once known as the **Kremmin Continuum,** and the dreaded planet of ultimate punishment, **Karakorum.**

THE NEGATION

Appolyon (species unknown) was once Charon's most trusted ally. Nearly as powerful as the god-emperor himself, Appolyon was banished from Negation Space for opposing Charon's conquest of the universe.

Charon (species unknown) is the god-emperor of the Negation. The full extent of his powers is beyond measure. He believes himself a benevolent ruler, and will stop at nothing to "improve" the lives of his subjects — whether they want him to or not.

Proconsul Gorg (Senkiemi/deceased) commanded the Negation garrison on the frozen world of Senkiem. His pious devotion to Charon put him at odds with the secular Komptin, who eventually ended his life in single combat.

Gullit (Kaliman Retriever) is Komptin's pet "dog." One of a breed of very intelligent, very vicious canines, Gullit was kept in isolation until Komptin picked up his pet to assist in the hunt for Kaine.

High Castellan Komptin (Kaliman) was a career soldier climbing the ladder in the Negation military hierarchy. He commanded the Prison World where Kaine and the others were incarcerated, then watched his career go up in smoke when his prisoners escaped. He now hunts Kaine in a singleminded quest for revenge.

General Kryzorr (Core Negation) is among the highest ranking military officials in the entire Negation power structure. Cool and calculating, Kryzzor has faithfully served his emperor since the first days of the Imperium.

General Murquade (Core Negation/deceased) was the vainglorious hero of the Negation military. His overconfidence proved his undoing when he single-handedly took on Samakar's army of empowered Australians.

Qztr (Lawbringer) is the most feared of Charon's cosmic enforcers. His curiosity about Evinlea's power has brought him into repeated personal conflict with Kaine's fugitives, several of whom he killed effortlessly.

Appolyon

Charon

Proconsul Gorg

Gullit

High Castellan Komptin

General Kryzorr

General Murquade

Lawbringer Qztr

CROSSGEN COMICS®
GRAPHIC NOVELS